MINIFIGURE
MAYHEM

by Beth Davies and Helen Murray

Penguin
Random
House

Senior Editor Helen Murray
Editor Beth Davies
Designers Sam Bartlett and Jenny Edwards
Pre-production Producer Marc Staples
Producer Lloyd Robertson
Managing Editor Paula Regan
Managing Art Editor Jo Connor
Publisher Julie Ferris
Art Director Lisa Lanzarini
Publishing Director Simon Beecroft

First American Edition, 2019
Published in the United States by DK Publishing
1450 Broadway, Suite 801, New York, NY 10018

Page design copyright © 2019 Dorling Kindersley Limited
DK, a Division of Penguin Random House LLC
19 20 21 22 23 10 9 8 7 6 5 4 3 2 1
001–313780–May/2019

A catalog record for this book is available from the Library of Congress.

ISBN: 978-1-4654-8355-3 (Paperback)
ISBN: 978-1-4654-8356-0 (Hardcover)

DK books are available at special discounts when purchased in bulk for sales promotions,
premiums, fund-raising, or educational use. For details, contact:
DK Publishing Special Markets, 1450 Broadway, Suite 801, New York, NY 10018
SpecialSales@dk.com

Printed and bound in China

A WORLD OF IDEAS:
SEE ALL THERE IS TO KNOW

www.dk.com
www.LEGO.com

Contents

OUT OF THIS WORLD

Aliens, monsters, and other magical minifigures live happily together.

I SAY ... F-L-Y! YOU SAY ... FLY-FLY-FLY!

IS THAT A NEW POTION, PROFESSOR?

YES. BUT IT HAS SOME UNUSUAL SIDE EFFECTS!

ZOMBIE TIMES

BRAAAINS!

Mini Facts

Likes Striped socks

Dislikes Getting broom-sick

Favorite animals Bats and cats

Wacky Witch

Life is no fairy tale for the unlucky Wacky Witch! Her grumpy cat is too busy napping to help the Witch with her spells, and bugs keep eating her gingerbread house!

WHAT IS A WIZARD'S FAVORITE SCHOOL LESSON?

SPELLING!

Muddled magician

The wise old wizard has read every magic book in the land and has a potion to solve every problem. If only he could remember where he left them all …

Zombie Businessman

Everything this Zombie does is slow! He struggles to get up when his alarm clock rings. He walks to work slowly. His coffee is always cold because it takes him so long to start drinking it!

WHAT DO YOU CALL A SLEEPY MONSTER?

A ZZZZZZZOMBIE.

Full of cheer

Unlike the Zombie Businessman, the Zombie Cheerleader has plenty of energy. She shows up to support her school sports teams at every game. Go Zombies!

Mini Facts

Likes Weekends

Dislikes Urgent deadlines

Favorite newspaper Zombie Times

Mini Facts

Likes Helping those in need

Dislikes Evil villains

Sidekick An enchanted singing sword

Elf Maiden

The Elf Maiden does not want to stay hidden in the Elflands. She is on a quest to find adventure! This brave hero journeys around the land armed with her golden sword and shield. Her pointed ears never miss a cry for help.

WHAT IS THE FIRST THING ELVES LEARN IN SCHOOL?

THE ELF-ABET!

Friendly face

The Faun fills his forest home with music. His favorite instrument is a flute. This odd creature has the body of a man, but the legs and horns of a goat.

Square Foot

Who is the mysterious Square Foot? People say he is a huge, hairy monster, but all they can ever find is his big, square footprints. This gentle giant really just wants some peace and quiet to practice his photography.

> HOW DO SNAKES SIGN THEIR LETTERS?
>
> WITH LOVE AND HISSES!

Ssshh, sssnakes!

Unlike Square Foot, Medusa finds it very hard to stay silent. She tries to sneak up on people and turn them into stone, but her hair is made of loud hissing snakes!

Mini Facts

Likes Nature and wildlife

Dislikes Buying shoes

Favorite accessory Digital camera

CHALLENGE!

Stack a minifigure

See how many minifigures you can stack before they tip over! Try stacking against the clock or challenge a friend.

I HOPE MY FLIPPERS DON'T FALL OFF!

Look for studs that can be used to join minifigures together.

WHAT A WORKOUT!

Use small LEGO® pieces to connect your minifigures.

Start with a base plate. The smaller the plate, the harder the challenge!

15

Likes Solving problems

Dislikes Boring hair colors

Weapon Duo-fusion blaster

4-9

Cyborg

The fierce-looking Cyborg was an ordinary human before she was upgraded with advanced technology. She now has fast reflexes and amazing computer abilities. The only thing she fears is running out of power!

> WHAT IS A ROBOT'S FAVORITE SNACK?
>
> COMPUTER CHIPS.

Mega mech

Cyborg's friend Laser Mech is the coolest robotic hero in the universe. He even plays his own awesome theme tune.

Alien Trooper

The poor Alien Trooper has been asleep for many, many years. He has woken up and discovered that all of his advanced technology is completely out of date. He cannot conquer the galaxy now—but at least he had a good rest!

WHY DID THE ALIEN GO TO THE DOCTOR?

HE LOOKED A LITTLE GREEN!

Big name

This alien leads a huge interstellar empire. Her minions are not allowed to speak her name out loud (which is good, because it is very long and hard to say).

Mini Facts

Likes Taking over new worlds

Dislikes Alarm clocks

Weapon Laser blaster

Mini Facts

Likes Making spider decorations

Dislikes Websites crashing

Favorite accessory Her spider-silk cape

Spider Lady

Forget bats—this vampire loves spiders! Her castle is full of pet spiders and she makes her clothes from sticky spider silk. Spider Lady really likes the Fly Monster, but he avoids all her invitations to come over for a bite.

WHY DID THE VAMPIRE GO INTO THE CAVE?

TO HANG OUT!

Fly Monster

This creature was an ordinary fly until he was turned into a half-fly, half-minifigure hybrid. He is terrified of spiders!

Monster Scientist

The Monster Scientist is always experimenting and inventing new things, from rocket-propelled shoelaces to wacky monsters. He even experimented on his own brain to make it bigger ... but it just made him sillier than ever before!

WHAT DID THE SCIENTIST CALL HIS LATEST CREATION?

A MONSTER-PIECE!

Plant Monster

Monster Scientist gave his houseplant too much of an experimental plant food. It soon sprouted arms, legs, and a monster appetite!

Mini Facts

Likes Being praised

Dislikes Safety warnings

Favorite creation Fly Monster

BUSY MINIFIGURES

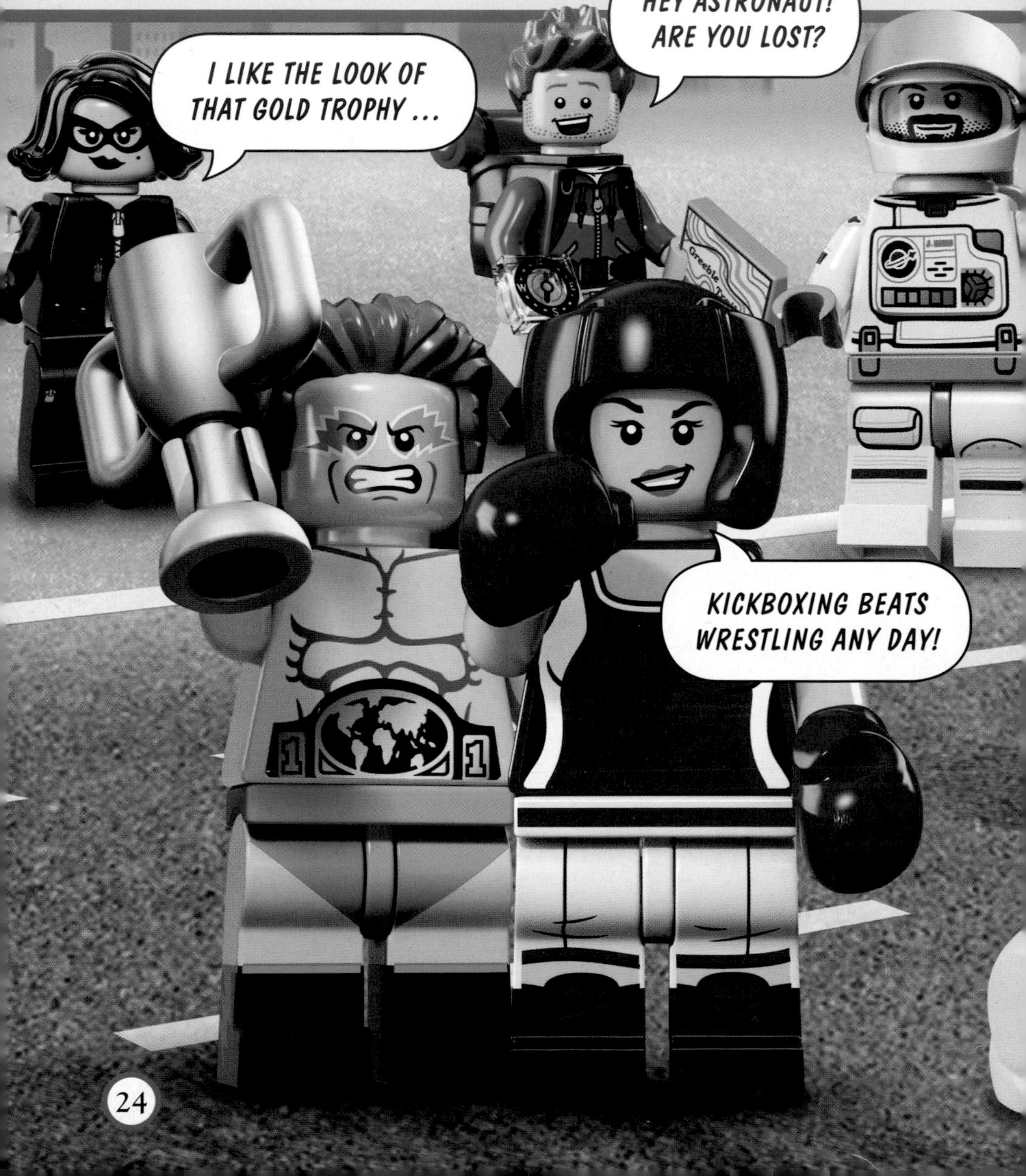

Minifigures are an active bunch! They have busy jobs and lots of hobbies.

WATCH OUT! COMING THROUGH!

THERE'S A SPEED LIMIT YOU KNOW!

I'VE NEVER SEEN A CITY SHARK BEFORE ...

WOW! MY COSTUME MUST BE GOOD!

Astronaut

This daring guy has spent his whole life dreaming about going into space. He built toy spaceships and read every book about space he could find. He eats special space food, even when he is on Earth. Now, he is ready for blast off!

> **WHAT DO ASTRONAUTS EAT THEIR DINNER ON?**
>
> **FLYING SAUCERS!**

What if … ?

Bang! The Scientist loves mixing things together and seeing what happens. Every experiment teaches her something new—even the ones that go wrong!

Mini Facts

Likes Building LEGO rockets

Dislikes Small meal pouches

Favorite subject Engineering

Likes New places

Dislikes Cold hands

Favorite animal Sloths—they are good at staying still!

Wildlife Photographer

The adventurous Wildlife Photographer travels the world to get the perfect picture. She has been to hot savannas to see lions and to chilly Antarctica to see penguins. She sets up her camera and waits … and … waits and waits. Click!

WHAT IS A RABBIT'S FAVORITE TYPE OF MUSIC?

HIP HOP!

Helping hand

If an animal needs help, call the Vet. She will check a rabbit's hearing, give a giraffe a neck rub, or even clean a crocodile's teeth!

Police Constable

The Police Constable is patrolling the streets. He watches out for trouble wherever he goes. The police officer says a cheery hello to everyone he meets—unless they are committing a crime!

WHAT DID THE POLICE OFFICER SAY TO HIS BELLY?

YOU ARE UNDER A VEST!

On the run

Look out, Constable! The Jewel Thief breaks into buildings to steal priceless gems. Unfortunately, she is also good at breaking out of jail!

Mini Facts

Likes Well-behaved people

Dislikes Dirty marks on his uniform

Favorite accessory Truncheon

CHALLENGE!

Guess who!

Choose a minifigure and see how quickly your friends can guess which one you have picked. They can only ask questions that can be answered with "yes" or "no"!

Take turns to choose a minifigure or ask the questions.

NO!

YES!

"IS YOUR MINIFIGURE DRESSED AS AN ANIMAL?"

Pick a character that might be hard to guess.

YES!

Hide your minifigure out of sight!

Roller Derby Girl

This daring speedster never slows down—on or off the track. Her speed is useful when dashing and dodging around her rivals, but sometimes she cannot stop. She once found herself halfway across the world!

WHY ARE MOUNTAINS SO FUNNY?

THEY ARE HILL AREAS!

Greeble Trail

Happy hiker

The Hiker loves being outdoors. Nothing dampens his cheery mood, even getting lost in the middle of a rainstorm!

Mini Facts

Likes Winning a roller derby game

Dislikes Traffic jams

Best friend Race Car Guy—he shares her need for speed!

Mini Facts

Likes Doing tricks

Dislikes Dry land

Favorite animal
Sea turtle

Professional Surfer

This talented surfer has won every competition that he has entered. Now, he tests his surfing skills against the best athletes in the ocean—dolphins, manta rays, and flying fish!

> WHY DID THE SHARK CROSS THE OCEAN?
>
> TO GET TO THE OTHER TIDE!

Fish out of water

This quirky guy used to be terrified of sharks, until he learned what amazing creatures they are. Now, sharks are his favorite animals!

Kickboxer

Kickboxing combines powerful punches and quick footwork, so the tough Kickboxer's feet are as quick as her fists! She once tried combining other sports, but no one wanted to play swim-tennis or go jog-bowling with her!

HOW DO YOU INVITE A WRESTLER TO A MATCH?

GIVE THEM A RING!

Loud and proud

The Wrestling Champion is very proud of his achievements and wants everyone to know it. Every time he wins a match, this show-off shouts about his victory!

Mini Facts

Likes Being active

Dislikes Tying shoelaces
with her gloves on

Favorite color Bright red

Minifigures love to party with their friends. It is time for a celebration!

KEEP ME AWAY FROM THOSE BALLOONS!

WHAT A BEAUTIFUL COSTUME!

DOES THIS PARTY HAVE SNACKS? I'M HUNGRY!

THIS IS THE BEST PARTY EVER!

Hot Dog Man

Everyone knows that Hot Dog Man loves hot dogs! He loves them so much that he has made his very own hot dog costume. His favorite type of party is a summer barbecue with—you've guessed it—lots of hot dogs!

WHY CAN'T THE MINIFIGURE RUN AWAY?

HIS FEET GET STUCK TO THE FLOOR!

Brick by brick

Brick Suit Guy likes to play speed building party games. Hopefully no one will think he is a real LEGO® brick and add him to their stack!

Mini Facts

Likes Hot dogs, of course!

Dislikes Spilling mustard

Favorite food Um ... hot dogs!

Mini Facts

Likes Giving gifts to her friends

Dislikes Balloons popping

Hobby Tying bows

Birthday Party Girl

This little girl loves balloons, cake, and party hats. When she finds the perfect gift for her friend, she opens and rewraps it again and again. She just gets so excited!

WHAT DID THE EGG SAY TO THE CLOWN?

YOU CRACK ME UP!

Clowning around

The wacky Party Clown can make any balloon animal that you could wish for ... as long as it is a dog!

Disco Diva

The Disco Diva is dressed to impress! She is always first onto the dance floor at parties. She likes to take control of the microphone, too. This superstar cannot help it—she was born to sing and dance!

> WHY DID THE SINGER CLIMB A LADDER?
>
> TO REACH THE HIGH NOTES!

Rock hard

Step aside, Disco Diva! The Rock Star is ready to perform his mega hit song "Brick Wall Baby." His fans are so excited!

Mini Facts

Likes Disco tunes

Dislikes The music being turned off

Favorite color Purple

Mini Facts

Likes Surprises

Dislikes Cleaning his clothes

Favorite cake Chocolate

Cake Guy

Surpriiiiiise! Cake Guy has been waiting to surprise everyone by bursting out of a cake! There is frosting everywhere, but luckily it is very tasty! Just how exactly did he fit into the cake?

WHY DID THE STUDENTS EAT THEIR HOMEWORK?

BECAUSE THEIR TEACHER SAID IT WAS A PIECE OF CAKE!

Perfect bakes

Every celebration needs tasty treats! The talented Gourmet Chef whips up cakes, pies, and cookies for all of her friends.

Minifigure muddle

Mix up the heads, torsos, and accessories of your minifigures. What is the most random character you can create?

Find minifigures with unusual costumes and accessories.

Cactus Girl

Cactus Girl thought her costume idea was fantastic, but now she keeps bumping into people and bursting balloons with her prickles. Her cactus arms also make it impossible to eat cake. Oops!

WHAT DID THE FLOWER SAY TO THE CACTUS?

YOU'RE LOOKING SHARP!

Beautiful bloom

Flowerpot Girl may seem shy, but she blossoms when she is having fun with Cactus Girl and her other cute friends.

Mini Facts

Likes Making costumes

Dislikes Ordinary clothes

Next costume idea Lobster (so she can pick things up!)

Mini Facts

Likes Winning prizes

Dislikes Slow coaches

Dream job Race car driver

Race Car Guy

3, 2, 1 … go! Competitive Race Car Guy always wants to be first in line for a slice of cake, first to open presents, and to win every party game. He just really loves winning!

WHAT DO YOU CALL A HORSE THAT LIVES NEXT DOOR?

A NEIGH-BOR!

Giddy up!

Is that a real horse? No, it is Cowboy Costume Guy and his clever party outfit! He loves telling silly jokes and horsing around.

Butterfly Girl

Happy Butterfly Girl loves bugs and hopes to get a job studying them one day. She shows her passion for insects with her pretty butterfly costume. She just wishes she could really fly!

HOW DO UNICORNS GET TO THE PARK?

ON A UNICYCLE!

Shiny happy unicorns

Unicorn Guy and Girl bring magic and adventure to everyone they meet. They also sprinkle glitter wherever they go!

Mini Facts

Likes All bugs

Dislikes Cold weather

Dream pet Caterpillar

Quiz

1. The Faun has legs like which animal?

2. Which minifigure has snakes instead of ordinary hair?

3. Which minifigure carries a duo-fusion blaster?

4. Who created the Plant Monster?

5. Where does the Wildlife Photographer travel to see penguins?

6. What is the Professional Surfer's favorite animal?

7. What color gear does the Kickboxer wear?

8. What does Hot Dog Man dislike?

9. What is the name of the Rock Star's hit song?

10. Which minifigure would like to have a pet caterpillar?

Answers on page 63

Glossary

Antarctica
A region of Earth that surrounds the South Pole
and is almost entirely covered by ice.

conquer
To take control of an area or group of people using force.

constable
An officer in the British police service.

engineering
The scientific study of designing and building machines,
buildings, and other structures.

experimental
Something which has not been scientifically tested and
may not work successfully.

gourmet
A person with excellent knowledge of food, or food that
is of a very high standard.

interstellar
Something that exists or happens between stars in space.

minion
A humble and obedient servant.

quest
A long or difficult mission to achieve something.

reflex
An action that does not require any thought and can be carried out at high speed.

savanna
A grassland area with few trees that is found in hot regions on Earth.

truncheon
A club or baton carried by police officers.

Index

Answers to the quiz on pages 58 and 59:
1. A goat 2. Medusa 3. Cyborg 4. Monster Scientist 5. Antarctica 6. Sea turtle 7. Red 8. Spilling mustard 9. Brick Wall Baby 10. Butterfly Girl

A LEVEL FOR EVERY READER

This book is a part of an exciting four-level reading series to support children in developing the habit of reading widely for both pleasure and information. Each book is designed to develop a child's reading skills, fluency, grammar awareness, and comprehension in order to build confidence and enjoyment when reading.

Ready for a Level 3 (Beginning to Read Alone) book

A child should:

- be able to read many words without needing to stop and break them down into sound parts.
- read smoothly, in phrases and with expression, and at a good pace.
- self-correct when a word or sentence doesn't sound right or doesn't make sense.

A valuable and shared reading experience

For many children, reading requires much effort but adult participation can make reading both fun and easier. Here are a few tips on how to use this book with a young reader:

Check out the contents together:

- read about the book on the back cover and talk about the contents page to help heighten interest and expectation.
- ask the reader to make predictions about what they think will happen next.
- talk about the information he/she might want to find out.

Encourage fluent reading:

- encourage reading aloud in fluent, expressive phrases, making full use of punctuation and thinking about the meaning; if helpful, choose a sentence to read aloud to help demonstrate reading with expression.

Praise, share, and talk:

- notice if the reader is responding to the text by self-correcting and varying his/her voice.
- encourage the reader to recall specific details after each chapter.
- let her/him pick out interesting words and discuss what they mean.
- talk about what he/she found most interesting or important and show your own enthusiasm for the book.
- read the quiz at the end of the book and encourage the reader to answer the questions, if necessary, by turning back to the relevant pages to find the answers.

Series consultant, Dr. Linda Gambrell, Distinguished Professor of Education Emirata at Clemson University, has served as President of the National Reading Conference, the College Reading Association, and the International Reading Association.